For David and Julie —

With very best wishes from

Tim Heath.

THE DRAGONS AT MARSHMOULDINGS

To Jonathan Meuli

The Dragons at Marshmouldings

Tim Heath and Tim Baker

PARVUS PULCHER EST

Allison & Busby
London and New York

First published 1984 by
Allison & Busby Limited
6a Noel Street, London W1V 3RB
and distributed in the USA by
Schocken Books Inc.,
200 Madison Avenue, New York, NY10016

British Library Cataloguing in Publication Data
Baker, Tim
　　The dragons of Marshmouldings.
　　I. Title　II. Heath, Tim
　　823′.914 [J] PZ7

ISBN 0-85031-535-2

ACKNOWLEDGEMENTS:
To Andrew Eames, Louise Scull, Michael Andrews,
Rachel Heath and the Haymarket Theatre, Leicester.

Set in Century Schoolbook by
Top Type Services Ltd., London EC1
Printed in Great Britain at The Pitman Press, Bath

1 Marshmouldings Hall

Once upon a time, in the heart of the English countryside, there was a house called Marshmouldings Hall and it was the biggest house in the world. Since the reign of William the Conqueror it had been the home of the Lords of Marshmouldings, who in the past had been very wealthy. Over the centuries, as each Earl in turn had added on yet another wing, the house had grown.

The present Earl, however, was not quite as rich as his ancestors. Lord Moufflon de Moule, the 17th Earl, could hardly afford to live in the house with a skeleton staff of two, let alone make it any bigger. In actual fact, it was as much as he could do to stop it from becoming any *smaller,* for every so often reports would reach him of how yet another part of the building was falling down or sliding away.

Money was needed urgently and many times the Earl had been advised to open the house to the public. His Aunt Nancy, who occasionally came to stay at the Hall, was constantly telling him that this was the answer to all his problems.

"But Aunt dear," Lord Moufflon would say, "there's nothing here for the public to see. The interesting collections have all been sold and we don't have a zoo or a model railway or anything."

And so the Earl had lived in the Hall all his life with an elderly housekeeper called Mrs Lott and a faithful butler called Soames.

One morning, the front door bell rang. It was a builder making enquiries. He had been waiting for some time when the door was opened by Soames the butler.

"Good morning, sir. Can I help you?"

"Oh yes," said the man. "You see, it's about my friend. He came to count the bedrooms last week and we think he may have got lost. Mind if I have a quick look round?"

"Not at all, sir. Please come in," said Soames. "Perhaps I could be of assistance in showing you over the house?"

"Oh no, it's all right. I can find my own way, thanks. Won't be a minute," said the man, who had already disappeared.

Soames said, "Very good, sir" and returned to his duties.

Now the 17th Earl spent his time in the nursery wing at the top of a spiral oak staircase at the end of the Long Gallery, next to the chapel and the manuscript library and overlooking the vegetable garden. It took Soames half an hour to reach his master from the front door.

"Oh hello, Soames," said the Earl, looking up from his paper.

"As I was saying, my Lord, before I answered the bell, we really should have a map of the building. The housekeeper tells me that lodgers have been found in the Tapestry Room."

"Good gracious, Soames. Did she call the police?"

"They were the police, my Lord. They had lost themselves investigating the burglary."

"The burglary?"

"The theft of the stud box from your Lordship's bedroom," Soames prompted.

"Ah yes," the Earl recalled, "I think I remember reading about it in the newspaper. I'm not as out of touch as you think, Soames."

"No, my Lord."

The Earl looked at Soames and Soames looked at the Earl and silence followed. The Earl was in fact very out of touch indeed. The house he lived in was so enormous that he might as well have been living in a world of his own. What went on in the outside world was a total

mystery to him, for although he read the newspapers, his butler would often remind him that reading about the world was not the same as living in it.

"I read, Soames," the Earl announced, "that that hamburger fellow has had to close all his restaurants."

"Indeed, my Lord?"

"Apparently, he can no longer afford to heat the food," the Earl explained. "Perhaps you'd care to see the article?"

Soames raised an eyebrow but only close examination would have revealed which one. His eye caught the headline:

HAMBURGER EMPIRE COLLAPSES
MacRelish forced to close due to rising fuel costs.

"I don't understand it, Soames. Kingly MacRelish is one of the richest men in the world."

"So I believe, my Lord, but the world is a much colder place outside."

The Earl glanced quickly at his butler and said: "I can't believe it's as cold as this room, Soames. Couldn't we have the heating on just a little bit? It's all very well saving money, but this time I really do think that we've gone too far."

"The heating *is* on, my Lord."

"Is it really? Oh dear, Soames, I'm so sorry. Is it really? I'm so out of touch now...I think I'll take a walk in the garden."

"Very good, my Lord," said Soames, "will that be all?"

"Yes, I think so, thank you. Oh no, there was one thing," the Earl went on. "I've had a letter from Mr Warmington. He's back from his holiday in America and he's coming to tea tomorrow."

"Tomorrow, my Lord?"

In all his years of service at Marshmouldings, Soames had only twice had cause to question his position in the house. He had found himself in a wardrobe one day, upside down, and for the first time in his life had asked himself the question: "Why am I here?" Nobody had told him about the secret trapdoor. The second occasion was when he had learned that the Earl had a friendly neighbour called Mr Warmington, who happened to be a dragon.

"A dragon, my Lord?" Soames had enquired.

"That's right, Soames, a dragon."

The butler was always slightly nervous when he heard that the dragon was coming for tea. He went to tell the housekeeper but as he did so he shuddered to think what tomorrow might bring.

2 A Dragon for Tea

It was nearly tea time on the following day when his Lordship and Soames were examining the scarecrow in the kitchen garden. Suddenly, behind them, they heard a roar and there on the cabbages was Mr Warmington.

"Warmington, how lovely to see you again!" the Earl exclaimed. "And how was your holiday?"

"Not very happy, I'm afraid," the dragon boomed. "Lord Moufflon, I have some terrible news. You know my nephew Houston? He's disappeared."

"Disappeared?" the Earl echoed, looking very concerned. "But that's simply dreadful. You must come in, Warmington, and tell us all about it."

Afternoon tea had been served and, having kindled the fire and toasted the tea cakes, the dragon was settling down to his story. The Earl had lit his pipe and whenever he seemed to be falling asleep, to which he was often inclined in the afternoon, the dragon would wake him with a sharp breath of steam.

13

"I wish you wouldn't do that," the Earl would complain. "You do make me jump sometimes."

"But you're not paying attention," Warmington would grumble. "Now listen."

The dragon had arranged to meet his nephew in the car park at New York airport. When Houston had not been there, Warmington had flown on to Dragon Island, which is where most of the world's dragons live (although only dragons know exactly where it is). The last time that Houston had been seen there, however, was when he had left for New York. Smoke signals had been put out all over the world but no one had seen the missing nephew. Perhaps he had been careless and had crashed into an aeroplane. Perhaps he had got lost in the city or perhaps he had been kidnapped. But who would want to kidnap a dragon? Dragons had no money. An enormous tear slid down Warmington's face as he looked beseechingly at the Earl.

"Please help us, Lord Moufflon," the dragon sniffed. "We asked the police in New York to help us but all they said was: 'Don't waste our time, baby. We've got enough on our hands without looking for dragons.' They suggested we try Disneyland."

"I do understand," said the Earl sympathetically. "I don't suppose many people believe in dragons nowadays. Oh Warmington, what can we do?"

"Come with me to Dragon Island," Mr Warmington replied. "I can take you on my back. We can start a search from there."

"But what about Soames?" said the Earl. "I couldn't go without him, you know."

It was impossible for the dragon to carry them both so the Earl gave the matter some thought and at the same time rang for his butler. In the time that passed while they waited for Soames, something like memory stirred in the breast of his Lordship. He remembered the dragons of his youth and the adventures of his ancestors....

"Soames," cried his Lordship, when the butler arrived, "we must help Mr Warmington to find his nephew. We are travelling to Dragon Island and shall need the balloon. Can you remember where it was put?"

"It hasn't been used since the fifteenth Earl's expedition to the Andes, my Lord, but I believe it was stored in the attic of the North-West Wing."

"Run and fetch it, there's a good chap," said the Earl. "Tell Mrs Lott we're leaving, pack a trunk for us both and we'll meet you by the South-West Terrace."

Soames bowed and departed without even raising an eyebrow.

"How can I ever thank you?" the dragon cried.

"Don't worry, old boy," the Earl assured him. "We'll find your nephew. About time I did something useful; haven't seen the outside world for ages — not since Aunt Nancy's ball."

The dragon was going to thank him again when the

15

Earl said: "My dear fellow, I'd save your breath. You'll need it to blow up the balloon."

One hour later, a remarkably quick time for anything to happen at Marshmouldings Hall, they had all met by the South-West Terrace. The Earl had written down the dragon's directions to the island and Soames had brought the balloon from the attic. His Lordship climbed into the basket and while Soames held the balloon down, Warmington began to puff. Soon the enormous ball was full of the dragon's fiery breath and

16

the Moufflon "M" on the balloon's outside looked splendid in the afternoon sun.

"Come on, Soames," the Earl called, "pass the trunk."

Soames complied and then climbed on board. Inside the basket they had to shout to make themselves heard above the noise of gases.

"Thank you, Warmington, you can let go now!" the Earl cried.

"My Lord, we seem to be rising," Soames remarked.

With a farewell shout the dragon flew off and the balloon was away. As they rose in the air, his Lordship and Soames looked over the edge of the basket. They were above the chimneys now. Higher and higher they went and again they looked down.

It was the first time that anyone had seen all there was of Marshmouldings Hall and the Earl gasped.

"My word," he said, "it looks like a city."

3 Disaster in the Air

Almost immediately, high above the chimneys of Marshmouldings Hall, disaster struck: they had forgotten the instructions for working the balloon. The basket had been searched but all in vain.

"But I thought you'd packed them, Soames," said the Earl.

"I did, my Lord."

"Well they're not in the trunk, Soames."

"No, my Lord, they were packed in a special pocket on the bottom of the basket. I thought your Lordship had taken them out."

"No, I haven't taken them out, Soames. I didn't even know they were there. On the bottom of the basket you say?"

The Earl looked at Soames and Soames looked at the Earl: his Lordship was not pleased.

"I am terribly sorry, Soames, but there is only one thing to do. Since we must have the instructions, you must climb out and get them from the pocket."

18

"Yes, my Lord."

"I shall hold on to your heels."

"Thank you, my Lord."

Gingerly, Soames leant over the side of the basket. The Earl took hold of his heels and gradually eased the butler's body over the edge. Soames became conscious of the wind in his ears. Marshmouldings Hall swam beneath him as the basket rocked from side to side.

"Now hold on, Soames," his Lordship yelled.

Slowly but surely, Soames crept nearer to the bottom of the basket, his hands clinging on to the rope around the edge. He reached out towards the pocket.

"How much more?" the Earl called out.

"Just a little further, my Lord."

And then the basket, which had been rocking madly with so much weight on one side, gave a sudden lurch. It was as much as the Earl could do to stop himself from falling out and it was only when the basket had settled again that the Earl was aware of something: he was no longer holding Soames's heels.

"Soames," cried the Earl, "where are you?"

"Still here, my Lord," came a shout from beneath, "but I require assistance."

Soames was hanging on to the edge of the basket by a rope at the bottom, having turned a somersault just like an acrobat. "I'm not very sure, my Lord, that I can hold on much longer. May I suggest that you land the balloon?"

"But I don't know how, Soames," the Earl wailed, beginning to panic. In vain he looked in the basket. There were various strings and an anchor, but what they were for he had no idea.

"Oh why did we leave in such a hurry," he cried, "and why did I ask Soames to climb out of the basket? I should have known he would never refuse." He looked in dismay at all his belongings: the trunk, the provisions, his umbrella, which they'd remembered to pack at the last minute. He seized the umbrella.

"Here Soames," the Earl shouted, holding it over the side, "hold on to this and I'll pull you up."

"Oh thank you, my Lord," the butler gasped, as with first one hand, and then the other, he took hold of the handle. The Earl had to lean out further and the basket rocked again. Try as he might, the umbrella was slipping from his Lordship's hands....

"You must let go, my Lord," Soames urged. "Don't worry about me—" and with that he was gone, umbrella and all.

At once the balloon gained height with the loss of a passenger and Marshmouldings Hall grew smaller. His Lordship tumbled backwards, but as soon as he was able to stand again, he peered over the edge.

Roads, trees and cottages had taken the place of park and gardens and as he had expected, Soames was nowhere to be seen. The balloon flew on, out of control, and the Earl looked sadly at the floor of the basket.

Later that day, a lighthouse keeper was amazed to see a hot air balloon sail over his lighthouse and out to sea. He could have sworn that he had heard a voice shouting "Help" and he called to his daughter to turn down the radio, so he could hear what the man was saying.

"But Dad, it's Woody and The Wormies," the girl called back and by the time the record was over, it was too late. All they could hear was the sound of the sea and the gulls.

In the balloon itself, as night drew on, his Lordship wrapped up as best he could. He was shocked and tired. He wished Warmington was there and Soames too, of course. He would never be able to forgive himself for what had happened to Soames. Dragon Island seemed so far off that he had practically forgotten all about it. Fortunately, the balloon was looking after itself. The wind had slackened, the sky was clear and, thanks to the heat of the dragon's breath, there was no chance of the balloon sinking into the sea. When disasters had happened at Marshmouldings Hall, Soames would say that it would all seem better in the morning. Remembering that Soames was usually right, the Earl fell asleep.

4 Friends in the Right Places

Soames was falling to certain death: he had to think fast.

"Perhaps if I open the umbrella," he thought, "it might break my fall. But on the other hand, it might break the umbrella — such a pretty one, too, from Mr Smith's in London. His Lordship would be furious. It was a present from his Aunt Nancy and he was very attached to it. But there again, he could always buy another...."

After much debate, he came to a decision. He decided to open the umbrella...

As Soames sailed sedately overhead and gently landed on the tiles beside them, a stork and her family, who lived on the roof of Marshmouldings Hall, looked on in wonder.

"Who's a lucky boy then?" the stork remarked.

Soames was too dazed to reply. The process of decision-making while falling from the balloon had almost been too much for him and he sat down on the tiles to collect his thoughts. One thing was certain. The Earl was in danger and had to be rescued.

"What are you going to do now then?" The stork had spoken again.

"I need to get word to the dragon," said Soames.

"The dragon?"

"Yes madam," Soames went on, "it is most important. By the way, my name is Mr Soames. I'm the butler here to Lord Moufflon."

"And who's he then?"

"Your landlord, madam," Soames explained.

"Oh really?" said Mrs Stork. "That's nice."

"My dear madam," said Soames, "I was wondering if you could possibly tell me the quickest way down to the ground?"

"Well, it could take you days," said the stork, "or even months, if you happen to get lost."

"Oh dear," the butler agreed. "You're quite right of course."

It began to rain. It was only a shower but the tiles and ledges would be slippery for hours and far too dangerous to climb. Now there was nothing that Soames could do, at least not for the time being. Who would hear if he shouted for help? To cheer himself up, he started to sing: "'se vuol ballare, signor Contino; se

25

vuol ballare, signor Contino—'".

"Of course, I could always get my Kevin to take a message," the stork suggested.

"Oh madam, could you really?" Soames cried thankfully. "What a marvellous idea. His Lordship

26

would be so grateful. You shall have to come to tea downstairs one day. Please ask your son to be as quick as he can. The life of his Lordship is almost certainly at stake", and he gave Mrs Stork the directions to Warmington's cottage. Kevin flew off and Soames settled himself as comfortably as he could while Mrs Stork made him a cup of tea. They could only wait and hope for the best.

It had seemed like hours when Kevin returned. Soames had been asleep and it had now grown dark.

"He's coming, Mum," the little bird shouted excitedly, pointing a wing at the sky, "he's coming."

Out of the dark came the eyes of the dragon, a gigantic flame and finally a familiar voice: "My dear Mr Soames, I hope you are not injured. Good evening, madam, your son has been most helpful."

"Thank you, sir," said the stork. "Cup of tea?"

Alas, they could not stay. As soon as it was light, it would be vital that they went in search of the Earl. They thanked the stork and her family again and Soames climbed on to Warmington's back.

Carefully avoiding the chimneys, the dragon took off and over the South-East Wing they flew. Gables and turrets passed beneath them but still they flew on until they spotted the roof of the wing where Soames had his quarters. There they landed and Mr Warmington spent the night on the butler's sofa.

Soon after breakfast the following day, they started

their search by flying towards the coast, hoping that the
Earl might have managed to steer the balloon in the
right direction for Dragon Island. It was not long before
they were flying past a lighthouse.

"Look dear," called the keeper's wife, "it's a dragon!"
Her husband rushed outside.

28

"A dragon?" he queried, looking up at the sky. "Oh yeah, so it is." And they went back inside to watch television.

Mr Warmington flew onwards out to sea but still there was no sign of the balloon.

"Perhaps we should make enquiries," Soames suggested. "Look, Mr Warmington, there's a ship down there, do you see?"

The dragon flew downwards and soon they were alongside the vessel, whose name was *Maid of the Mud*. When they were close enough, Soames called out to the men on deck: "Have any of you gentlemen seen a balloon?"

"A what?"

"A balloon!"

"If you're looking for Lord Moufflon, we've got him here," came the answer. So the Earl was safe.

"Oh thank you, thank you," Soames called back in relief. "May we come aboard?"

"Be our guests."

It was only when the dragon flew closer that they saw, flying from the stern, a skull and crossbones flag. The *Maid of the Mud* was a pirate ship.

5 "Maid of the Mud"

"It's a trap, Mr Soames," the dragon warned.

"But, Mr Warmington, the Earl is there. How would they know we were looking for him otherwise?"

Soames was all for going aboard but the dragon was suspicious. He looked again at the pirate ship. It seemed so old and small as to be hardly capable of sinking a rowing boat let alone an ocean-going liner. He couldn't even see any cannons. The crew looked as if they had escaped from a circus and no one appeared to be doing any work.

"They're not pirates," the dragon thought, "they must be actors making a film or something." He circled once around the ship and then landed. Just at that moment, his Lordship himself appeared on deck as the crew gathered round.

"Soames and Warmington," the Earl cried joyfully, shaking their hands, "thank goodness you're safe! Let me introduce you to our pirate friends. I told them to keep a lookout for you."

Soames, however, was far more interested in how his Lordship came to be there.

"Well," the Earl explained, "this morning I decided I simply had to learn how to work the balloon. So I prised up a floorboard in the bottom of the basket using the tip of the anchor and then I was able to reach the instructions. I'm terribly sorry, Soames. I don't know why we didn't think of that yesterday, frankly." (There was an awkward pause while his butler coughed and then the Earl continued.) "Anyway, as soon as I had read the instructions, I was able to land when a ship came in sight."

The dragon looked about him. "And this is the first ship you saw?" he said.

"That's right," the Earl stated proudly, "and isn't it splendid? A genuine nineteenth-century pirate ship, I'd say. Now let me introduce you to the crew. They've been so kind."

One by one he presented them starting with the captain, whose name was Bosseyed. The mate, for some reason which the Earl could not grasp, was called "Just-

31

Done-Time" Jules and the name of the cook was Growbag. The bosun's name was Skid.

"And that is our ship's boy, Lenny," the captain announced, pointing to a youth who was hanging out the washing. "Welcome aboard, gentlemen! Now what's all this I hear about a 'dragon island'?"

Warmington looked at the Earl sharply.

"I told them we were looking for your nephew, Warmington," the Earl said, producing a piece of paper from his pocket, "and I was just about to show them your directions."

Suddenly there was a burst of flame from the dragon's mouth, gone in a second but it had done the trick. The piece of paper was burnt to a cinder. The dragon apologized, explaining that a cough had been troubling him for days, but the captain went pale all the same.

"Rollmop!" the captain barked. (Rollmop was an unseen steward.) "On deck immediately and clear up this mess! I don't think this sea air can be good for a cough, gentlemen. Perhaps you would care to join us for lunch," and he led the way below.

All through the meal, the dragon was uneasy. He wanted to ask what the pirates did, if they were pirates at all, but something about the captain made him afraid.

"Perhaps it would be better to say nothing," the dragon thought, "and leave after lunch." When they had finished, he looked hard at the Earl and explained the situation to the captain.

"You've been so kind," said the Earl after Warmington had finished. "I'm sorry that we have to rush off like this but we really mustn't keep you from your work. Perhaps we should go and inflate the balloon again?"

"Of course, Lord Moufflon, we quite understand," the captain smiled and they all went on deck together.

To the Earl's surprise, when the captain told Lenny to fetch the balloon, the boy did not move but stared at them with a sheepish grin.

"Well jump to it, Lenny," the captain crackled. "Where have you put it?"

There was a whining note in the boy's reply. "Fell overboard, sir," he said.

"Just slipped from your hands, I suppose?" the captain sneered knowingly.

The boy could hardly stop giggling. "Yes, sir."

"Stand back," the dragon thundered. Somehow he had known all along. His breath was ablaze and some

rope caught fire. Again he shouted: "Lord Moufflon! Soames! On my back! Quick!"

But everything happened too fast. The captain and the mate had caught them from behind and were holding pistols to their heads.

"Put that fire out, Skid," the captain ordered, "and watch that dragon. Breathe again, Warmington, and these two go."

34

His Lordship and Soames struggled in vain but were soon tied up by the ship's boy. The bosun had produced a fire extinguisher and had put out the blaze. Now he pointed it at Warmington.

"Who are you people?" the Earl stammered. (Soames had fainted.)

"You'll find out below," the captain answered. "Jules, Skid, take them below to cabin number two."

Soames was revived and all three were taken down to the second cabin, which was quite unlike the rest of the ship. It had neither furniture nor windows and was completely sealed, apart from a vent in the ceiling. Strangest of all were the walls, which seemed to be covered in a white dust, except in one corner where the wall was black.

The reason for this was soon clear. In the same corner lay the huddled form of a small dragon. Whoever these pirates were, they had found Houston.

6 "Green Agro"

When Soames and the Earl had been introduced and it was discovered that Houston was unharmed, Warmington asked him about the pirates.

"Why, Uncle, didn't they tell you?" Houston sobbed. "They're not pirates at all. They're dragon hunters."

Warmington stared at his nephew in amazement. "I

don't believe it," he laughed nervously. "How do you know?"

"I heard them talking," said Houston. "We're on our way to join another ship and they asked me the way to our island. I didn't tell them though and there was nothing they could do. They were given instructions not to touch me."

The evening before his uncle was due to arrive, Houston had been walking down a street in New York when a green van had pulled up suddenly beside him. Four men had got out and, throwing a fireproof blanket over his head, had bundled him into the back. No one had seen or heard anything and the van had driven off.

"The next thing I knew," Houston concluded, "I was in this cell."

Warmington snorted angrily at the wall which immediately went black with the heat of his breath but refused to burn.

"I believe it must be made of asbestos, Mr Warmington," Soames remarked. "We have it in the kitchen at home."

But the dragon was not even listening. With all his might he blew against the wall, vainly trying to set it on fire. Eventually, he fell back exhausted.

"It's asbestos, Warmington," said the Earl gently. "It doesn't burn."

"But everything burns if you set it alight," the dragon cried.

"But not asbestos," the Earl persisted. "It was a brave attempt but I fear these hunters have thought of everything." His Lordship patted the dragon kindly and shook his head.

While our friends below could only worry and wonder, the crew on deck were hard at work. The *Maid of the Mud* had gathered speed and was sailing as fast as her engines could drive her.

Captain Bosseyed was pacing the deck. He stopped beneath the bridge, looked at his watch and then called to the mate: "Rendezvous in three hours, Jules. Keep her steady."

"Aye aye, captain."

Then Skid the bosun arrived. "Can't we change now, skipper?" he grumbled. "I'm tired of looking like a pirate."

"But it suits you, Skid," said the captain.

"Come on, skipper, give us a break."

"Very well," the captain agreed, "but stay out of sight until it gets dark," and he continued pacing up and down. It had all gone too far, this pirate game, he decided. Fancy having a private yacht that was made to look like a pirate ship! He had heard that playing pirates was The Boss's hobby, but this was ridiculous. Perhaps The Boss had never grown up, or was mad. The captain was looking forward to joining the *Green Agro*. Now there was a *real* ship, or so he had heard. He looked again at his watch and decided that there was time for him to go below. He would change as well.

In the fireproof cabin, the time passed slowly. The dragons were asleep and the Earl had been thinking.

"This whole thing is like a horrible dream, Soames," he said, breaking the silence.

"If only it were, my Lord."

"Do you think we shall ever see Marshmouldings again?"

His butler could not answer.

"If I'd known that the world was going to be like this," the Earl complained, "I should never have left home." He had never been so unhappy in all his life.

Soames reminded him that they could hardly have refused to help the dragons.

"Yes, Soames, I know, but we've found Houston now and I want to go home."

Just then, the cabin door opened and in walked the captain, followed by Lenny and the bosun. There was something extremely unpleasant about their appearance: they were all carrying guns and wearing bright red overalls.

"On deck all of you," the captain barked.

Soames and his Lordship stood up at once, hardly believing that these were the pirates that had given them lunch. Warmington and Houston were still asleep so Captain Bosseyed gave them a kick.

"How dare you?" the Earl cried, stepping up to the captain. But before he could do anything he was seized by Lenny, and now the dragons were awake.

"What's going on?" said Warmington.

But all the captain would say was: "We want you upstairs."

Night had fallen and it was cold on deck. In the glare of floodlights, the sea swirled around them for hundreds of yards.

"Perhaps we're meeting the other ship," whispered Houston to his uncle.

"What ship?" Warmington asked.

And then, as if in answer to the dragon's question, there was a rumbling noise and everyone on board looked out to sea. Louder and louder it grew and then all of a sudden, a volcano seemed to be erupting beneath the waves. The water bubbled as, with majestic slowness, something like a shark's fin rose up from the surface of the ocean. But it was larger than a shark's fin and soon it had become like the summit of a mountain. Slowly, while the rumbling deepened to a roar, another one appeared, then another and then more. From what seemed like the middle of a thousand cascades appeared cannons and control towers, radio masts and missile launchers, lights without number, deck upon deck of them as the giant wall of metal and light slid slowly past them and upwards. The bubbling subsided and so more became visible and soon it was so vast that the pirate ship was completely dwarfed.

Nobody on board the *Maid of the Mud* had seen the

Green Agro before and they craned their necks to take in all of it. They gazed in silence and then they heard a voice, booming across the water: "Good evening, Captain Bosseyed, and congratulations. Three hostages in one day is excellent work."

The Earl looked at Soames and Soames looked at the Earl, while the dragons shivered. Thundering through the night, the voice came again: "Mr Warmington, you have a choice before you. Unless you tell us the exact location of Dragon Island, Captain Bosseyed will shoot the butler. If, after that, you should still be unco-operative or have told us a lie — for we shall check what you tell us on our charts — Captain Bosseyed will shoot his Lordship. Is that quite understood? Bosseyed, get ready, and give the dragon a loudhailer."

The captain obeyed and Warmington stood there, looking at Soames.

7 Life on the Ocean Wave

It was now the following day. The Earl and Soames had been cast adrift in a lifeboat.

The sun beat down and the sea heaved beneath them and all they could hear was the churning of water and the creaking of timbers. Images and memories of the night before kept flooding back and would leave them exhausted as they tried to understand how they were still alive. Neither of them had slept and neither of them had said a word to each other since dawn. Suddenly the Earl spoke.

"I do think it was awfully mean of them to leave us like this," he said.

"Indeed, my Lord, but if I may say so, it is better than being shot through the head."

There was no denying that Soames was right, so the Earl was silent and continued to row. His butler was endeavouring to steer with the tiller but for all they knew about navigation, they could easily have been travelling in circles. After a while, the Earl spoke again.

"Soames?" he said.

"Yes, my Lord?"

"Wouldn't you say it was four o'clock?"

"I really wouldn't know, my Lord."

"I'd say it was time for a spot of tea, Soames, wouldn't you?"

The hunters had made one mistake. They had forgotten to remove the tin of rations and can of fresh water that were stored on board. There was also a box containing mugs, plates, knives, forks, spoons and a saucepan. The great find, however, was a tiny gas stove and a box of matches: not quite what his Lordship and Soames were used to, but they had soon grown accustomed to their change of lifestyle. To begin with, in order to save them, they had not so far eaten any of the rations. But as it was over a day since their lunch on the *Maid of the Mud*, what the Earl had suggested seemed a splendid idea.

"My Lord," said Soames, when the water had boiled, "tea is served." With consummate skill, he put a little dried milk and a teabag into two mugs and then added the hot water. "Will you take sugar, my Lord?"

The Earl answered, "Yes please," and Soames added the sugar. Then, with a spoon, he extracted the teabags and carefully placed them in an empty mug.

44

"I trust that you will excuse me, my Lord," Soames ventured, "if I take the liberty of stirring your tea?"

"My dear Soames, it's not as if we were at Marshmouldings now, you know."

"My Lord, indeed not," Soames replied stiffly as he stirred the tea and passed it across to his Lordship. The Earl took the proffered mug and sipped the tea gingerly.

"Perfectly delicious," he sighed. "There wouldn't be something to go with it, would there?"

"My Lord, I am sure that you will appreciate," Soames explained, "that the choice is limited to ship's biscuit only. But, happening to remember your Lordship's partiality for strawberry jam, and remembering too that I had forgotten to include some in our box of provisions...." With the care of a conjurer, he extracted a jar from the pocket of his coat.

"Oh Soames, you are wonderful!" his Lordship cried and soon they were enjoying what both of them agreed was the afternoon tea of a lifetime.

Unfortunately, however, it was soon over and when Soames had washed the tea things, it was time to consider their situation. They had calculated that they had just enough food and fresh water to last them for three days.

"I hope you will not mind my saying, my Lord," Soames remarked, "that it would be a very good thing if we were to be rescued."

"But what about Warmington and Houston and all the other dragons?" said the Earl.

What could poor Warmington have done but direct the hunters to Dragon Island? Sitting in the lifeboat, the Earl and Soames had watched in horror as the *Maid of the Mud*, with everyone on board, had been hoisted onto the *Green Agro*, which had then disappeared beneath the waves.

"My Lord, there is nothing that we can do for them now," Soames urged. "We do not know where the island is and even if we did, we have no means of navigation."

There was a pause while the Earl gave the matter some thought.

"I have it," he cried. "We simply must be rescued."

"Yes, my Lord."

With Soames's help, his Lordship hit on the brilliant idea of lighting a fire in the ration tin to attract the attention of passing ships. Gathering together as much rubbish as they could, and hacking away little pieces of wood from the boat itself, they removed the rations from their tin container and filled it up with what they had gathered. Match after match went out before they could manage to light the pile, but suddenly there was a tiny flicker of flame.

"We really must have smoke, Soames," the Earl wittered impatiently. "They'll never see us otherwise."

Soon they discovered that by putting the lid of the container over the fire, they were able to build up smoke which could then be released by taking the lid away again.

It was much harder work than his Lordship realized. He scanned the horizon again and again but not a single ship sailed into view. What would his Aunt Nancy have said if she could see him now?

Suddenly, he did catch sight of something but it disappeared immediately. "I thought I saw something there," he mused, and looked again.

It *was* there. The Earl had seen a puff of smoke.

"A ship!" he cried and nearly fell overboard as he jumped for joy. There was another puff, quickly followed by another. It was undoubtedly a ship just below the horizon. The Earl sat down and began to row as hard as he could.

"Soames," he ordered, "keep the fire going. We're going to catch that ship if it's the last thing we do. You never know, we might be in time after all."

8 Technology at Work

Hundreds of fathoms beneath the sea, the *Green Agro* sped effortlessly onwards. From the sealed window of an asbestos crate, Warmington could see the hunters working in the huge control room as they kept their course for Dragon Island. He knew that they would have found the island sooner or later. As The Boss had remarked through the ship's loudspeaker: "We have the technology, dragon." Warmington recalled that his only friends were miles away or possibly drowned and his heart sank lower and lower.

Captain Bosseyed passed the window and glanced in to smile provokingly. He was looking forward to seeing some action and had just arrived at the control room console when a ship's corporal stepped to his side. Through an intercom system in the door of his crate, Warmington could just catch what they were saying.

"We've sighted land, sir," the officer confided. "Would you care to take a look?"

Captain Bosseyed walked over to the periscope.

"So this is Dragon Island?" he murmured. "Well, well, well — and they don't even know we're here. Thank you, corporal, that'll be all."

"What are you going to do, you cowards?" Warmington roared so that everyone in the control room turned round to listen.

"Now calm down, dragon," the captain ordered. "We want them alive. We're just going to put them to sleep, that's all."

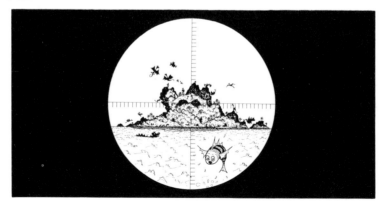

"And what do you mean by that?"

"Well, I suppose there's no harm in telling you now," the captain said with a smug leer. "We're going to wait until dark and then, when your friends are sleeping, we're going to flood the island with gas. That'll keep them snoring for the whole of tomorrow. They'll all be asleep when we move in."

"Cowards!" the dragon roared again but the captain had walked away. "Cowards!"

Late that night, according to plan, miniature submarines approached the island and released a gas which floated in on the waves. Four hours later, precisely on schedule, the infra-red scanners were able to report a state of slumber amongst the dragons.

And then, eventually, the sun rose and morning came. Dragon Island had never seen anything like it: men everywhere in asbestos suits and all along the beaches, sleeping dragons being wheeled on trollies into landing craft. The hunters worked in teams of ten, systematically combing the island. Armed with rifles, loaded with darts that would put even the strongest dragon to sleep, they were totally prepared for any emergency. Enormous fire engines stood by, eager to extinguish the tiniest flame while helicopters, littering the sky, fetched and carried in gigantic nets.

The day wore on. Like a lazy monster being fed by servants, the *Green Agro* wallowed in the bay as landing craft after landing craft deposited its load of

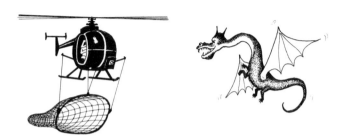

captive dragons and returned to the island for more. It seemed that nothing could stop the operation for even a minute, or so the hunters thought. They had not noticed the two men in a rowing boat that had nearly reached the shore.

"Hurry Soames!" said one of the men. "We're nearly there!"

"Very good, my Lord," said the other faintly, paddling hard.

The Earl and Soames had arrived. The smoke that they had seen below the horizon had not been a ship at all but a smoke signal from the island itself. A dragon had spotted the fire in their boat and had mistaken it for another dragon. Now, as the beach grew nearer and the water shallow, the Earl leapt into the sea, waded on to the dry sand and charged towards the nearest group of hunters.

"STOP!" he bellowed.

"Oh dear," muttered Soames, quickly climbing out of the boat and following after the Earl, "I'm not sure that his Lordship really knows what he's doing."

"STOP!" the Earl bellowed again and this time a dragon stirred. A hunter fired immediately and instantly drugged by the dart, the creature was still again, but the noise of the gun had woken two more dragons. Shouting and yelling like a madman, the Earl ran between the hunters and over to a line of trollies: "Wake up, wake up!" he cried.

A fire had started and soon there were hunters running in all directions. There was a jet of water and the fire went out but another had started further off. Over by some trees, another dragon was moving and waking his neighbour. An engine was pumping fiercely but could hardly keep up as, little by little, the number of fires increased. Suddenly a dragon flew up into the air.

"Don't shoot!" cried the Earl from the middle of the chaos. "Oh please don't shoot. Come on Soames, there's a whole family over here."

"Coming, my Lord," Soames shouted from behind a rock. He had just found a baby dragon all on its own.

"Now stop this, all of you," his Lordship pleaded, as he struggled bravely with one of the hunters. "This is simply disgraceful so stop it at once."

Groping his way through the smoke, Soames had just rejoined the Earl when they were both knocked over by a stream of water. When they came to their senses, they realized that the hunters had taken them prisoner. They had caused a fair disturbance between them but now the *Green Agro*, with its water cannons, began to soak the island. Across the sky, dragons that had tried to fly away were quickly caught in the helicopters' nets. No one was hurt and not a single dragon had been killed, but all hope of rescue was at an end.

"All right, you two," the captain barked, as Lord and butler stood sorrowfully before him, "you're going to meet The Boss."

54

9 The Pirate King

Led by the captain and carefully guarded, the party entered the bowels of the *Green Agro*. Like the doors that opened and shut automatically, nearly everything they saw was a fire precaution. Extinguishers stood on every corner and smoke detectors blossomed on every ceiling. The ship was not made entirely of asbestos for its dust eventually would have poisoned the air and every so often they passed a dial on the wall which showed the balance of atmosphere components. Everything sounded a smooth "swish" punctuated only by the "bleep" or "click" of wall-to-wall gadgetry. In every room, in every lift and on every moving staircase, music played with melodious monotony, occasionally broken by the soft reminder of the ship's loudspeaker: "Ladies and gentlemen, the leisure and recreation centre on deck five is now open. Thank you."

The Earl was about to look at Soames when the same voice was heard again: "Service Two Thousand to Dragon Checkpoint Three, please, service Two Thousand to Dragon Checkpoint Three. Thank you."

Wet, dirty and very unhappy, the prisoners were taken down corridor after corridor. Suddenly, Soames was puzzled by the passage that stretched in front of him. He felt that he had been in this place before. With all its stairs and its countless rooms, the ship seemed rather like home.

"I wonder where all the dragons are?" the Earl whispered.

"I presume that there must be dungeons down below, my Lord." Soames felt a shove in the back.

"Silence, you," came a voice from behind, "we're here."

Soames was silent. These hunters had no manners, he thought.

They had stopped before a black door on which was painted a skull and crossbones. Beside it on the wall was a security camera, eyeing them suspiciously.

They waited.

The camera completed its inspection, the door opened and the Earl and Soames were led inside.

The apartment in which they found themselves was very large and quite unlike the rooms through which they had just passed. It had been made to look like the captain's cabin of an old-fashioned ship, with oak

panels and brass lanterns. One end was a window, through which they could see an expanse of ocean and the other was a bookcase, lined with editions of *Treasure Island*. Around the walls hung portraits of famous pirates, and dotted about there were tables laden with treasure. But the object that really dictated the atmosphere was a stainless steel desk that stood in the middle of the room, covered with switchboards and microcomputers. Behind it, smoking a cigar, sat The Boss himself.

The Earl gasped as he peered through the haze and recognised a face that he had often seen in the papers. It was Kingly MacRelish, the hamburger baron.

"Pleased to meet you," The Boss smiled, extending a hand. "I'm Kingly MacRelish."

"I know," the Earl retorted but before he could say anything else, the man before him had jumped from his chair and started to sing: " 'For I am a Pirate K-I-N-G!' "

" 'You are — hurrah for our Pirate King!' " the captain and the guards chorused and then there was silence.

Kingly MacRelish was seated again and calmly blowing cigar smoke.

"You may be wondering why I did that," he said quietly. "Shall I tell you?" (The Earl and Soames nodded slowly.) "Right then — well you see, as a boy, I always wanted to be a pirate but Daddy wouldn't let me. My father was a butcher and used to make me work in his shop. But I had *always* wanted to be a pirate, *always*."

"I know what you mean," the Earl put in, "I wanted to be one too when I was a boy."

"And what did your parents say to that?" MacRelish asked.

The Earl beamed and said: "Well it's a long time ago now, but I rather think they gave me a pirate suit for my birthday."

Kingly MacRelish glared at the Earl and quivered violently. Leaning forward across the desk, he breathed cigar smoke into his Lordship's eyes. "Well there you are then, see?" he growled. "I wanted a pirate suit more

58

than anything else in the world but I didn't get one, did I?"

"Oh dear, I am sorry," the Earl mumbled and Soames looked sympathetic.

"I've got one now, though," The Boss continued, "and I've got a pirate ship all to myself. Oh yes, I became a butcher and look what happened. Invented the hamburger takeaway, didn't I? I've got them all over the world now."

"But didn't I read that you had closed them down?" the Earl recalled. "Something to do with the cost of heating?"

"That's right," said Kingly MacRelish, standing up and walking to the window, "and I'll tell you why, shall I? Why? Because what the world needs now, Lord Moufflon, is energy. Everybody's looking for it, everywhere: energy from under the ground or under the sea; energy from atoms or the sun's rays and the cheaper it is, the better." He paused to control his excitement before turning and saying: "And *I've* found it, Lord Moufflon, I have found the cheap alternative."

The Earl went pale. He was slowly beginning to realize what Kingly MacRelish was saying.

"I think you know what I mean, Lord Moufflon," The Boss smiled. "I'm talking about the dragons. Now I know you'll say that I'll never get away with this. But who's going to stop me?"

This was more than the Earl could stand and he was

59

about to flare up angrily when Soames interposed with: "Mr MacRelish, you were about to say?"

"Nobody believes in dragons now," MacRelish affirmed. "They don't exist for most people. Besides, when I put this lot into my kitchens, I'm telling you, they're not going to look like dragons."

"You don't mean to say," the Earl trembled, "that you're going to mince them up and turn them all into burgers?"

Kingly MacRelish was patient.

"Not all at once," he said. "The babies will be kept until they've grown up, of course. We've lined up a ceremony to re-open the chain as soon as the ship docks. The moment that's over, we'll start the slaughtering. The 'Dragonburger'," Kingly MacRelish announced with pride, "will be fast food, faster than ever: the instant meal that saves energy at the same time. You see," he explained, settling once more in his armchair, "the special advantage of the 'Dragonburger' is that it will cook itself in its own heat. 'For I am a Pirate K-I-N-G!'"

"'You are — hurrah for our Pirate King!'" the chorus came again, stopping suddenly just as before.

Soames, who was trying hard not to feel sick, said: "Forgive me for asking, Mr MacRelish, but don't you think that the dragon meat will taste most unsavoury?"

"To be perfectly frank with you, Mr Soames," The Boss replied, as he lit another cigar, "I don't think anyone will taste the difference."

60

"But what will happen when the supply of dragons runs out?" the Earl pursued.

Kingly MacRelish leant back in his chair.

"Well," he drawled, "it won't be for some time as naturally, we'll be mixing the dragon with pure beef. Nobody will know exactly what they're eating. We might use your friends as an advertising gimmick but that'll be all the public will see of dragons. The supply will run out, certainly, but I think by then we'll have made enough money to look elsewhere for alternatives."

At that moment, a light winked on one of his switchboards. Kingly MacRelish picked up the telephone and listened.

"They've scoured the island," he reported, as he put the receiver back, "and we've got the lot. Thank you for coming to see me, gentlemen. In actual fact, I was wondering if you two would like to be waiters in one of the takeaways?"

The Earl looked at Soames and Soames looked at the Earl: they knew that they would have no choice in the matter. Soames shuddered as the vision of plastic dustbins, aluminium counters and strip lighting flashed before him and a never-ending line of small boxes trundled across his brain. The poor Earl could barely think at all. The fate of the dragons was terrible, simply terrible and when it occurred to him to think of his own predicament, another horrible thought crossed his mind. For who would live at Marshmouldings Hall now? As he looked across the desk at Kingly MacRelish, his eyes filled with tears.

10 World Events

At her home in London, the Earl's Aunt Nancy was horrified to read that nobody had seen her nephew for over a fortnight.

Lady Nancy lived alone with her two dogs. Since the death of her husband, she had devoted her energies to the running of charities and numerous committees. Her days were crammed with meetings and engagements and her evenings hardly ever saw her at home. Not even breakfast was a quiet moment in her busy life, for breakfast was sacred to the daily devouring of newspapers. Munching her toast with demonic fury, she would scan the articles with a roving eye, stopping whenever she came to an interesting passage. She would then summon her dogs and read the paragraph aloud to them. She had just discovered the story about her nephew.

"I hope you're listening, you two," she warned, peering over her spectacles.

The two dogs, whose names were Wagner and Mussorgsky, looked up while Lady Nancy read out the article: "...'as the search continues'," she concluded, "'police in Cornwall are currently questioning a lighthouse keeper'."

"Goodness gracious," she muttered, putting the paper down, "how simply frightful."

Lady Nancy was a woman of action. Leaping to her feet in a flurry of paper, she stormed imperiously out of the room and marched at once to the front door.

"MUSSORGSKY!" her Ladyship cried, "WAGNER? CAR! We're off to Marshmouldings to find that idiot nephew of mine. Heaven knows why they never installed a telephone."

Handbags snapped, the dogs scuffled and minutes later they were squashed inside her Ladyship's veteran sports car (a 1929 Fitzpetreau-Wingfield) and roaring along the Great West Road.

Of course, had Lady Nancy known the truth about her nephew, she would almost certainly have been flying to

New York. Many others were, for news that the
MacRelish hamburger chain was soon to re-open had
spread across the globe like wild fire. Scientists were
frantic with curiosity and the world of commerce could
hardly believe its ears. On the international stock
markets, the price of MacRelish shares soared and, to
add to the excitement, all New York was awaiting the
arrival of the *Green Agro*, Kingly MacRelish's ocean-
going liner. According to reports, it had now been
converted into the largest hamburger takeaway parlour
in the world; an enormous, floating restaurant which
Kingly MacRelish would open to the public the moment
the ship docked.

As the great day dawned, military bands were
already in position. Carloads of policemen lined the
waterfront and crews of engineers from the television

companies had set up their lights and cameras. Radio and pressmen were standing by: the media were having a field day.

By the quayside stood a large platform where the opening ceremony was due to take place and from its middle grew a thicket of microphones. Around its edge hung banners with slogans such as "Welcome back, Kingly" and "Guess who loves ya, burger boy". But all this was nothing compared to the appearance of the ship itself when at last it sailed into view.

Night had come and the sky was spangled with tiny lights. Flotillas of boats packed the harbour and the Statue of Liberty held up her torch as if to ward off the encroaching darkness. The city held its breath in anticipation. Was that it there? The *Green Agro* had entered the harbour.

Like a ghostly shadow, it hovered across the water in total silence. Onlookers were aware of a black presence floating towards them, but still there was nothing to see. The crowds were murmuring in disappointment when all of a sudden, the entire ship was a blaze of electric signs. Reds and yellows flashed alternately, bathing spectators in a throbbing orange, while pictures of dragons in neon green flared fantastically against the night. As the ship drew nearer, the applause grew louder and at once the bands began to play. Towering above the quay, the vessel came closer and soon it was moored beside the platform.

66

Plush in his evening dress and proudly smoking a cigar, Kingly MacRelish trotted in triumph down the thickly carpeted gangway. He stood behind the microphones and immediately the music stopped. Television cameras slid into place and pencils trembled over notepads, as the great man began to speak: "Mr Mayor, ladies and gentlemen, thank you for giving me such a great reception — I'm truly flattered."

There was loud applause and Kingly MacRelish cleared his throat. When the noise had died down, he continued: "As you know, the ever-increasing cost of energy forced me to close my hamburger operation. Quite simply, I felt that there had to be another way. And it is my great privilege tonight to be able to announce that I, Kingly MacRelish, have *found* that 'other way'."

"Mr MacRelish, can you tell us what that is exactly?" yelled one reporter.

"I think that would be telling, don't you sir?"

As laughter rippled through the audience, The Boss adjusted his bow tie. "Suffice it to say," he went on, "that as a result of research in my laboratories, we have come up with a process that will cook hamburgers more quickly, more cleanly and with less consumption of fuel than ever before. This is a process," The Boss persisted, raising his voice above the general hubbub of curiosity, "known only to myself and a handful of scientists. Its name is the 'Dragon' process and with it we shall make the fast food sensation of the century, the 'Dragonburger'! Yes, sir! These will be hamburgers as *you* know and love them, but simply cooked with our new technology. Ladies and gentlemen, I expect some of you are getting a little hungry, waiting for me to finish, so let's proceed with the ceremony."

He waved his cigar and a couple of waiters appeared, carrying a barbecue grill. If Lady Nancy had been watching television, she would have recognised the waiters as the Earl and Soames but as it was, they passed unnoticed. Sitting in a bun on top of the grill was a large burger, the last to be made of pure beef.

"And now," The Boss proclaimed, "to cook this hamburger for me, I should like to call upon a very special kind of chef."

A steel panel at the top of the gangway yawned open

and a dragon appeared in a chef's hat and apron.

"Ladies and gentlemen," MacRelish cried, proudly gesturing back at the ship, "Warmington the dragon!"

By now the crowd was hysterical, shrieking and pointing and hardly knowing whether to laugh or cry. Children jumped up and down, grown men fainted, women sobbed and the massed bands began to play

69

again. Mustering his dignity, Warmington walked down the gangway. He was trying to catch the Earl's eye.

"Now, Lord Moufflon," he whispered, as he stood on the platform, "speak to them."

The Earl looked round with a dull stare. "To eat here," he said, "or take away?" In the course of the journey, both he and his servant had not found it easy learning to be waiters in a takeaway kitchen, and as a result they had had to be brainwashed.

"Soames," hissed the dragon, "what's happened to the Earl?"

The butler grinned brightly and said: "French fries?"

Kingly MacRelish had waved for quiet and was now producing a flare gun out of his pocket. "Ladies and gentlemen," he announced, "just as soon as I have eaten this hamburger, which the good dragon is about to cook, I will shoot this flare. That'll be the signal for the opening of the kitchens and the start of the 'Dragon' process. Okay, dragon — fire away!"

Warmington pleaded desperately under his breath: "Help us, Lord Moufflon, please!" But it was clear from the expression on his Lordship's face that the dragons had been betrayed.

"Anything to drink, sir," the Earl replied, as if he had never even met the dragon, "or is that everything?"

11　Fast and furious

From within the ship, the hunters were watching as Warmington turned and faced the crowd. The gun had only to be fired for the first of the dragons to go to the slaughter.

The burger was waiting. Kingly MacRelish clicked his fingers at which Soames removed the bun and the Earl prepared the meat.

Now there was nothing that Warmington could do but move to the grill. Crouching down and opening his mouth, he started to breathe on the coals, gently at first but gathering quickly to an angry roar. All the anger that he had ever felt, and more besides, struggled from his lungs in rage.

The coals began to glow. Flames licked the grill and the spectators gasped in amazement. The meat sizzled, the fire crackled and the flames shot higher as Warmington roared with all his might.

"I must keep breathing," he thought, "I must keep

breathing. If I can't talk, I can still breathe and while I'm alive, I shall never stop breathing."

Never for one moment taking his eyes off the hamburger, Warmington roared as hard as he could until the burger was ready.

"Thank you, dragon," cried Kingly MacRelish, "that's great! Ladies and gentlemen, let's give our chef a big hand!"

Everyone clapped and two more waiters from the ship led Warmington back up the gangway. The smoke cleared but as Kingly MacRelish looked at the grill, it became apparent that something exceedingly strange had happened. It had nothing to do with the meat of the burger, which was one hundred per cent pure beef, but it may have had something to do with Warmington's feelings. Whatever it was, and nobody knew for certain, the colour of the burger had suddenly changed to a rich, emerald green.

Kingly MacRelish looked hastily at the audience and grinned.

"Magic fire," he explained, putting the hamburger into its bun, "but don't you worry: pure beef all the way. I'll just add some cheese 'n' tomato ketchup — there we go — and ummmn!"

There was a stunned silence while the world watched and listened. Kingly MacRelish was enjoying his food. Happiness and well-being oozed from his features, and as his jaws moved up and down, his eyes twinkled in pure contentment: all was well.

But no, all was not well, for he was mopping his brow and had started to belch. As the colour faded from his cheeks, his hands trembled.

"Ladies and gentlemen," he murmured, "excuse me please," and, rushing to the side of the platform, he was sick into the water.

There was another stunned silence and then everyone gradually began to laugh. Some of the crowd had walked away, hungry no longer, but most people stayed to see what would happen next.

Composing himself, MacRelish marched to the microphones. He tried to speak but the moment he did so, the laughter grew.

"I'll make them stop," he muttered furiously between his teeth and, pointing the flare gun into the air, he pulled the trigger.

BANG! it was heard by Soames, who started out of his trance. Running like the wind, he vanished up the gangway and into the ship.

BANG! it was heard by Captain Bosseyed in the office next to the dungeons.

"There's the signal, corporal," he grunted. "Tell the men to load their rifles."

BANG! it was heard by the Earl, who blinked and looked above.

"Oh, what a pretty star!" he thought, as he gazed at the flare wistfully, for it dazzled his eyes like the sun that he had seen one morning in the country. Slowly and gracefully the ball of fire flew over the ship, bringing to mind those wonderful creatures that his Lordship remembered from a story book.

"Look, Soames," he said, pointing to the sky, "a dragon!"

But his butler had disappeared.

The Earl looked frantically about, but all he could see were lights and faces and cars and lights and Kingly MacRelish, shouting wildly, and great tall buildings and men with guns, chasing Soames, and yet more faces and flashing colours and then it occurred to him that something was happening.

"SOAMES!" he yelled, "they're going to kill the dragons! RUN!"

But Soames was already out of earshot. Sprinting down corridors past other waiters, he had reached a lift in a matter of seconds but alas, it was out of order.

Regret : Elevator Malfunction!

"How inconvenient," he sighed, as the tramp of feet came ever closer, "I shall have to use the stairs" and so saying, he slid down the bannisters fifteen decks, spiralling downwards as if he were riding on a helter-skelter. It was only when he paused for thought at the bottom that he began to wonder where he would find the dragons. He had found himself in an empty passage.

"Now if this was Marshmouldings Hall," he panted, desperately trying to remember the only place he knew that resembled the *Green Agro*, "where would I go? Let me see...the lower conservatory would be over there, so I would have to cross the Rococo drawing room...".

In the vast gallery of asbestos dungeons, deep in the hold of the ship, the hunters were loading their guns. Captain Bosseyed was checking his list of dragons to be shot first: twenty in cell Z.

"...and through the Gothic banqueting suite," thought Soames, "which would bring me along by the Norman guardroom and down to the dungeon steps...".

The hunters had reached cell Z. Unlocking the door, Captain Bosseyed gave the command:

"Firing squad: form up!"

"Oh dear," said Soames, still puzzling his problem, "I hope this works."

Lightning never struck faster than Soames as he covered the length of the passage he was in, moving like a sprinter in the hundred metres. Racing round corners and vaulting over furniture, he never slowed down for a fraction of a second. Windows, doors, microwave ovens and deep-fat fryers flickered in the corner of his eye. Computer banks and baffled bureaucrats loomed large and disappeared as Soames sped onwards until he came to a flight of steps. Leaping from the top of it, he crashed through a door and there before him was the gallery of dungeons.

Unfortunately, however, cell Z was at the far end. "Firing squad: take aim!"

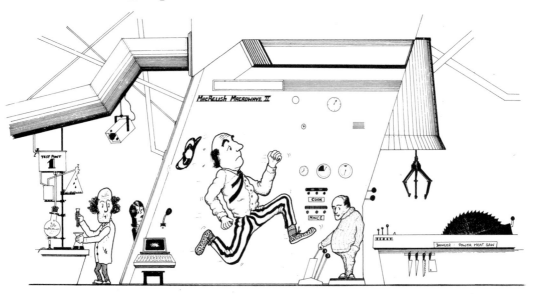

Soames kept running, his feet scarcely touching the ground. One by one, he passed the cell doors: A,B,C,D,E,F,G....

On the captain's command, the hunters lifted their rifles. Fingers on triggers, they waited for the order.

...H,I,J,K....

Cowering in fear, the prisoners huddled against the wall.

...L,M,N,O,P....

A dragon sobbed and tried to hide behind his paws.

...Q,R,S,T,U....

Another looked sadly at the hunters.

...V....

Taking a deep breath,...

...W....

...the captain...X,Y—and Soames had entered the cell, grabbed a rifle and was pointing it straight at Captain Bosseyed.

Everybody stood completely still and for at least a minute, nobody spoke a word.

12   On the Waterfront

Up above on the quayside, Kingly MacRelish was trying in vain to assure the crowd that nothing was wrong and was highly embarrassed when the Earl pushed his way to the microphones.

"Ladies and gentlemen, listen to me!" his Lordship shouted. "This man is a fraud. He plans to make dragon meat and turn it into hamburgers!"

The Chief of Police, who on seeing trouble had run up the steps of the platform, pushed the Earl aside. "What's the matter with you, kid?" he demanded. "Have you gone crazy or something?"

"Don't call me 'kid'," the Earl snapped, "my name is Lord Moufflon de Moule and if you come with me, I'll show you the dragons!"

"You mean to tell me that that was a *real* dragon we saw just now?" the officer asked, his face radiant with disbelief.

"Of course it wasn't, officer," MacRelish insisted, "it's just a thing we had flown out from Hollywood."

Suddenly, they heard the wail of a siren from within the ship and the voice of a terrified scientist crying out in alarm: "Mr MacRelish, Mr MacRelish — the monsters!"

"What monsters?" Kingly MacRelish shouted angrily.

"Mr MacRelish, the dragons have escaped!"

The wailing continued and men and women were scrambling along the decks in panic. Someone had lowered a second gangway onto the quay and down its steps fled cooks, pirates, waiters, cleaners, hunters, guards, laboratory assistants, engineers and what seemed to the Earl like the whole world — but there was no sign of Soames. Anxiously searching for his butler, the Earl spotted Captain Bosseyed who was waving his arms and shouting at the crowd: "get back, everybody, get back! They've set the ship on fire!"

Just as he spoke, there was a loud explosion and the sound of smashing glass. The crowd of onlookers and everyone on the platform ran for the cover of whatever they could find. As they turned to watch, the air was filled with dust and debris. The ship was no longer illuminated, but occasionally glimpsed through showers of sparks and the light of scattered fires. People were still flocking down the gangway. The last of them were making their escape in lifeboats or by jumping into the water.

"Oh dear," thought the Earl, "I do hope Soames is all right."

Kingly MacRelish stared in dismay as the *Green Agro* groaned and cracked in the ever-increasing heat. The fire brigade had just arrived but little could be done in the face of flames that were now themselves over fifty foot high. The firemen could only stand by as, very gradually, the sea began to do their work.

"Holy smoke," the Chief of Police gasped, "I guess you were right, Lord Moufflon. Look!"

But the Earl, who had seen already, was shouting "Hooray" and waving his arms, as out of the terrible glare of the fire came dragons, dragons and still more dragons. Black against the orange of the flames, they stretched their necks and spread their wings: babies clutching their mothers; fathers shepherding their families; grannies and grandpas coughing and choking as they stumbled through the smoke. Gathering together on the upper decks, they soared at once like migrating birds, those who could fly carrying those who could not. (There were also some who could swim but they had escaped already.) The ship sank lower and as the explosions continued, the fumes and steam billowed and belched from its blackened outside. The grids of neon fizzled and toppled. Radio masts crashed into the water and still there were fires raging. But the dragons were free.

"Excuse me, my Lord," said a voice next to the Earl.

81

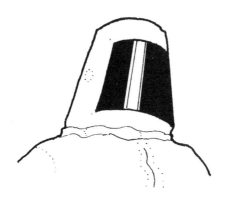

His Lordship, who had been busy watching the dragons, looked round quickly. "Soames," he said, "is that you?"

In front of him was a man dressed in an asbestos suit, complete with a masked helmet. The Earl was surprised. He was sure that he had heard the voice of his butler. Instead of answering, whoever it was removed the visor from in front of his face.

"Soames!" the Earl cried, "it *is* you! I was beginning to think you had perished."

"Not at all, my Lord, I am quite unharmed, I assure you. These fireproof suits are remarkably effective."

"But Soames, what have you been doing?"

Soames coughed gently and looked a trifle uneasy.

"My Lord," he said, "I am terribly afraid that I engaged in a slight altercation with Mr Warmington and Master Houston. I had only intended to set them free, but they would insist on what Captain Bosseyed was pleased to describe as, 'wrecking the joint'."

"Well, they certainly did something," the Earl replied.

"Yes, my Lord," said Soames, "I think they did."

"Well there we are," the Earl mused, "and the dragons are flying away. I would have liked to have said goodbye to Warmington and Houston but I don't suppose they want to see me now."

Again the butler coughed.

"My Lord, I trust that you will pardon my having taken a liberty...given the particular circumstances?"

"Yes, Soames?"

"My Lord, in view of the general situation, it seemed to me that the dragons would not be entirely safe if they returned to Dragon Island. Forgive me, my Lord, but I said that they could stay at Marshmouldings Hall, merely for the time being, of course."

"At Marshmouldings Hall?"

It was almost as if the Earl had forgotten that Marshmouldings Hall was his home. Slowly, he remembered the rambling passages, the countless bedrooms, the wings that were far too numerous to mention...there was certainly room for all the dragons.

"Soames!" the Earl exclaimed, regarding his butler with admiration. "What a simply *brilliant* idea!"

"Thank you, my Lord, but may I suggest that we discuss it later? I do believe I see Mr Warmington and Master Houston waiting over there to take us home."

Having made arrangements with the Chief of Police for a telegram to be sent to Marshmouldings Hall, they

83

hurried away to join the dragons and as they did so, the *Green Agro* turned over on its side and uttered a final hiss. All that was left of it now was a huge, steaming, burnt-out shell.

Kingly MacRelish turned aside. His mouth was twitching and his ears ached. "I don't want to be a pirate any more," he thought.

For the first time in his life, he believed in dragons.

Epilogue

Lodge gates creaking in the breeze; a drive that went on for ever and was filled with pot holes; birds twittering, the long grass shimmering...in the still tranquillity of the English countryside, Marshmouldings Hall was as peaceful as if nothing had happened throughout its history, the spirit of the Hall Oliver Cromwell had demolished the North Wing in a fit of pique.

The North Wing was only a ruin now but the rest of the house stood grand and serene, its towers and chimneys peeping in the sunlight above the trees. Occasionally, a battlement crumbled and here and there, a picture fell off the wall. But whatever had happened throughout its history, the spirit of the Hall remained unchanged. Battered idealism had kept alive a tiny flame: the spirit of kindness and hope that in the face of everything, had never been extinguished.

When Lady Nancy arrived from London, she had found the mansion full of police and newspaper men, all of them looking for clues.

The following morning, with the help of her dogs, she drove them out.

"OUT!" she screamed, brandishing a stick. In piercing tones she announced loudly that *she* would investigate the Earl's disappearance herself. Returning inside, she slammed the door and made her way to the Earl's study.

She was busy preparing her plan of campaign when Mrs Lott rushed into the room with a telegram. It read as follows:

EARL AND SOAMES SAFE AND SOUND STOP
RETURNING TOMORROW WITH DRAGONS STOP
PLEASE PREPARE BEDROOMS.

Lady Nancy glared at the housekeeper. "Who *are* these 'dragon' people?" she snapped.

"Beg pardon, my Lady, but I think they're friends of Mr Warmington."

"Mr Warmington?" her Ladyship roared. "Who *is* this Mr Warmington? And who, in Heaven's name, is *this*?"

A man had stumbled into the room; dirty, dishevelled and rather thin. It was the builder who had come, weeks before, to look for his missing friend.

"Mind if I come through?" he called, nervously wiping his feet on the carpet.

"It's quite all right, my Lady," the housekeeper explained, "we found some archaeologists here last week. Come on you," she said, turning to the man, "I think I'd better show you out. I hope you haven't been causing trouble."

Lady Nancy raised her eyes to the ceiling, as the voice of the builder drifted away: "... Well, I found this book, you see, in a big room full of them. Great story. All about knights of old, it was — really great. You see, there was this man and he...."

At that moment, a dragon flew past the window. Her Ladyship looked again and to her utter amazement, saw hundreds of dragons settling on the lawn. Others were still arriving. Some of them had landed in the trees, some more had landed in the flowerbeds and some were already playing in the fountain. The Earl and Soames, like runway officials at an airport, were waving them in to land.

Aunt Nancy jumped up and made her way to the Great Lawn as fast as possible. She ran to her nephew and gave him a hug.

"Muffles," she cried, "thank goodness you're safe!"

"Hello, Aunt Nancy," the Earl gasped, recovering from her python-like embrace, "how lovely to see you. Have you been here long?"

"I came down yesterday," her Ladyship explained. "The place has been full of police. We've been terribly worried about you both."

"I'm awfully sorry," the Earl said, hardly knowing where to begin. "Soames and I have had rather an adventure and all the dragons in the world have come to stay. They lost their home when the hunters invaded their island and Soames was brilliant and asked them here!"

With a puzzled frown, Lady Nancy looked at the guests, who by now were sitting patiently and waiting for something to happen.

"Moufflon dear," she said, "I don't think I quite understand who you mean by 'dragons'."

The Earl looked at Soames and Soames looked at the Earl. The Earl looked at Warmington and Warmington looked at Lady Nancy.

Slowly and graciously, her Ladyship smiled. "I think we can all be a dragon at times," she admitted.

"Dear Aunt, I knew you'd understand," said the Earl and then he remembered his good idea. It was a good idea that he had had for some time and now he was trying to remember exactly what it was. Not even Soames had heard it yet. Suddenly he remembered.

"Ah yes!" he exclaimed, climbing on to a garden bench. "Ladies and gentlemen, I am going to make a speech."

"Now quieten down, dragons," Aunt Nancy called and the Earl began.

His Lordship's speech was, in fact, extremely long but at the end there was loud applause.

"On behalf of us all," roared Warmington, "I should like to say that we think your idea is marvellous."

"Hear, hear!" cried a stout party at the back, while the baby dragons flapped their wings in excitement.

"We should only be too delighted," Aunt Nancy and Soames chorused.

"Oh thank you, thank you," the Earl sighed.

Lord Moufflon had suggested that, under the management of a charitable trust (The Marshmouldings Society for Prevention of Cruelty to Dragons), Marshmouldings Hall should be a dragon sanctuary. He had invited his Aunt Nancy to be Society President and his butler to be the Honorary Secretary. Warmington was proposed as Honorary Chairman and as Vice-Chairman, the Earl proposed himself. If the plan worked and the dragons were content, in a year's time the Hall and grounds would be opened to visitors on Saturdays and Sundays throughout the year.

"We might even make a little money by serving tea," he added.

Soames agreed that indeed this might be possible and as the Earl climbed down from the bench, he had never felt so happy in all his life.

"At last," he thought, "perhaps I have done something useful."

And so it was that the ancestral home was opened to the public for the first time. The dragons were extremely happy and the house was never cold again.

That night, tenderly painting the domes and spires a silvery grey, the moon rose over Marshmouldings Hall. His Lordship had gone to bed and Soames had retired to his quarters. A mouse was the only sign of life, as it scuttled to its home in the Minstrel Gallery. High among the chimneys, the stork was reading to her children before they went to bed.

Lord Moufflon could not sleep; a question had been nagging his brain for hours. He reached a hand through the embroidered curtains of his four-poster bed and pulled at a lever, bristling with rust.

Like the sound of a stone dropped to the bottom of a deep well, a tinkling was heard in the further reaches of a remote wing. Hours passed.

Eventually, the butler arrived. "My Lord?" said the voice of Soames in the gloom.

"Honestly Soames," said the Earl, who was still awake, "anyone might think that you have just had to walk five miles."

"I have, my Lord," the butler sighed.

"Oh Soames, I'm so sorry," his Lordship muttered, "I keep forgetting."

There was an awkward pause while the Earl considered the problems of distance at Marshmouldings Hall and then he spoke again.

"Soames?" he said, in a hesitant manner.

"Yes, my Lord?"

"Forgive me for asking, Soames, but where did you learn to run so fast?"

With a smile that nobody saw in the darkness, the butler explained: "I was once an Olympic Gold Medallist, my Lord, before I went into service."

"Really, Soames?" the Earl asked, immediately sitting up in bed.

"Because of the size of the house," the butler continued, "the then Lord Moufflon insisted that the servants were all good runners — including the ladies, my Lord."

"Including Mrs Lott?" his Lordship asked, his eyes widening in amazement.

"Indeed, my Lord, Mrs Lott is even faster than I am."

"Golly," the Earl gulped in wonder. "Does that mean you run all over the house now?"

"Only in emergencies, my Lord," Soames confessed, "for if I may say so, it ill behoves a butler ever to run."

The Earl thought this over very carefully.

"Well, it was certainly an emergency on board the *Green Agro*," he recalled.

Soames shuddered at the mention of the horrible ship and said: "My Lord, I would be grateful if we could never refer to that name again."

"No Soames, absolutely not," the Earl agreed and snuggled once more beneath the cover of his bed. "Good night, Soames."

"Good night, my Lord," the butler replied.

"Soames?"

"Yes, my Lord?"

"The outside world is not such a bad place after all, is it?"

"No, my Lord, indeed it is not," the butler admitted, as

he reached the bedroom door. He was just departing when the Earl's voice was heard again, murmuring drowsily.

"Good night, Soames," it said.

"Good night, my Lord," said Soames.

On the roof of the South-East Wing, the stork had finished her story and had come at last to the final words. She knew these off by heart and, without so much as a glance at the page, could inform her children, as she had done so many times before, that the characters of the story "all lived happily ever after".

"Oh mum!" the little birds whispered, looking up at their mother with wide eyes, "did they really?"

Mrs. Stork closed the book.

"Yes, my dears," she said, "they really did."